The BUDDIES

in

SOMEBODY'S

Story by
Brad Bluth

Illustrations by
Toby Bluth

HERO

Ideals Publishing Corporation

Milwaukee, Wisconsin

Copyright © MCMLXXXIV by Bluth Brothers Productions
All rights reserved. Printed and bound in U.S.A.
Published simultaneously in Canada.

ISBN 0-8249-8063-8

Dicky Duck, Jack Rabbit, and Bo Bo
are playing football in the schoolyard.

The ball gets stuck in the big oak tree
when Bo Bo kicks the ball hard.

"Wow! What a kick!" shouts Dicky.
"You sure sent that ball flying!"
Bo Bo starts to climb the tree, but stops
when he hears small voices crying.

He and his two friends listen
to sobs no louder than whispers.
And before too long the boys catch on
to the tears of the three Wren Sisters.

They hear Mother Wren has no money
for the payment on their loan.
And Rig E. Pig who owns Pig E. Bank
is soon to take their home.

"We won't let him!" Bo Bo shouts
as he falls from the tree to the ground.
Dicky and Jack, from behind the tree,
quickly come running around.

The Wren Sisters are taken by surprise.
They've never been seen so low.
Embarrassed that someone knows their plight,
they say, "No, please go, please go."

"I'll box Rig's ears," Bo Bo shouts,
"and pull his curly tail!"
"Now stop!" says Jack. "If you do that,
we'll all end up in jail."

"Look, Dicky." Jack Rabbit points
to a sign from Rig Pig, that scamp.
It reads: Cash prize for a foe who can go
nine rounds with JUNIOR CHAMP.

Then Bo Bo feels on each shoulder
the hand of a friend and a friend.
Jack and Dicky say they've a solution
and Bo Bo's services they extend.

They show Bo Bo and the Wren Sisters
Rig's poster on the tree.
Bo Bo brags, "Nine rounds with Junior Champ?
I'll knock him out in three!"

MEANWHILE, downtown at Rig's office
foul plans are being laid.
They don't call this pig "Rig" for nothing.
He's having the odds slightly swayed.

He is meeting with the fight promoter
who also referees —
a fellow of questionable honor
by the name of Rim Rat the Weeze.

This crook has come up with a boxer
and he calls him his "Junior Champ!"
But this Junior Champ is a junior bull.
Any foe Champ can easily stamp.

NOW, through the bank door rushes Bo Bo
with Dicky and Jack close behind.

"I've come to sign up for the big prize fight.
I'm the best boxer you'll ever find."

Bo Bo signs on the line and off the three go
as the sly Pig winks at the Weeze.
"No problem," sneers Rat, "Champ will knock him out.
He'll beat this monkey with ease."

Determined to win, brave Bo Bo trains
before school, at noon, and at night,

Punching a bag, jumping rope, and eating big lunches to build up his strength for the fight.

The Wren Sisters stitch star-spangled boxers
with white stars on a waistband of blue.
Bo Bo checks out his red and white stripes in the mirror,
and it's clear he's impressed with the view.

What a confident air is reflected there.
The Wrens' woes he's sure to relieve.
But when he meets Champ, the junior bull,
he will see he's been very naive.

At last, the night of the big fight arrives.
There's excitement in the air.

Jack and Dicky tend Bo Bo's corner.
Bo Bo waves to the Wren Family there.

The school gym is crowded with people.
The bleachers to the top are full.
The Weeze announces, "Rig Pig's Junior Champ!"
and out steps a Great Big Bull.

Jack and Dicky gasp, "Oh, no!
Let's call this off right now!"
But Bo Bo's determined to save the Wrens' home.
"It's the only way I know how."

Though Bo Bo is scared, he knows he must find
some way to last the nine rounds.
The fight is announced. The boxers shake hands.
And the bell for round one sounds.

The bull advances. He smiles at his foe.
Then he swings to punch Bo Bo out.
Bo Bo dodges and ducks. And each time the bull misses,
the crowd lets out a big shout.

The monkey moves fast for the first three rounds,
and he's very rarely hit.
But in four, five, and six he slows at his tricks;
and by eight he gets hit quite a bit.

"Let's get on with this," snaps the Weeze to the bull,
"Rig E. Pig just gave me a wink.
It's time for you to knock this kid out.
Rig Pig's getting edgy, I think."

The bull attacks. He whacks and smacks.
He punches out Bo Bo's left light.
The monkey's down, the monkey's up.
He's determined to last the fight.

Bo Bo is battered. He's beaten in the ninth.
His spirit has taken a crunch.

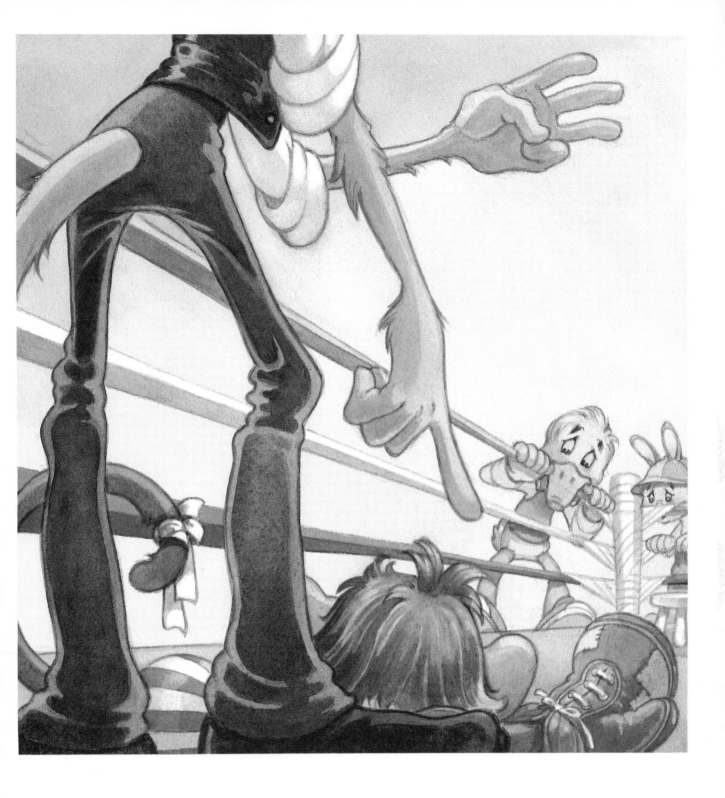

The bull, with a grin, lifts the kid's chin
and delivers the knock-out punch.

The crowd gives a moan as Bo Bo falls,
and the count is begun by the Weeze.
Somebody's Hero is down on the mat,
one eye closed but the other eye sees.

He sees the Wren Sisters, who beg him to stop,
standing in front of him there.

He remembers that day at the foot of the tree
when he told them not to despair.

Up, up, up the Weeze goes,
round and round;
then down, down, down
by Rig Pig on the ground.

The Weeze grabs the pig
with a desperate clasp,
and Rig E. Pig goes up
with a squeal and a gasp.

Pig, Weeze, and ropes wind
like a big ball of string
round the bull who falls flat
on his rump in the ring.

In nine rounds the bruised monkey
hasn't hit the bull once.
Now there the bull sits
like a big dazed dunce.

So Bo Bo winds up
and he hits the bull's eye.
Then the bull snaps to and snorts,
"You're gonna die!"

Bo Bo streaks down the aisle
Through the door and outside.
The bull's in pursuit
with Rig and Rat for the ride.

"Jack!" screams Dicky,
"What do we do?
The bull's after Bo Bo
and he might get him too!"

In a flash Jack grabs a rope
with a hook tied to one end.
He ties the rope tight to the platform
and hands the hook end to his friend.

The raging bull is charging
strapped with flailing Pig and Weeze.
Jack grabs the boxer's waistband,
and Dicky hooks the bull with ease.

The tension mounts — then slows and stops;
the bull train's at the door.
Bo Bo's outside. The bull? He tries,
but can't take one step more.

The bull looks back at what could snap —
it's the waistband of his britches!

Then back he slides. He grabs both door sides.
Now the audience is in stitches.

The monkey's face appears
below the bull's arm in the door.
And Bo Bo's smile at this pig pile,
turns the laughter to a roar.

Then Bo Bo draws back for the final attack,
and SNAP the pig pile goes.
Was it Bo Bo's blow or did the bull let go?
Nobody really knows.

They rocket through the ceiling,
then through the stratospheres.
The crowd goes wild with laughter
as the pig pile disappears.

Bo Bo is the champion.
And because he won the fight,

the Wren Sisters and their Mama
have a place to sleep tonight.

Now Dicky, Jack, and Bo Bo
did what buddies could do.
When somebody needs a hero,
that hero can be you.